The V... Mannered Penis

How a penis can have a happy stress-free life

Sylvia Clare

With illustrations by

David Hughes

Please write a review
on Amazon if you
like this book.
Thank you
(Please leave back at stable when finished)

Introduction

A book about the Penis.

Why would we need a book like this?

Why write this book now – there are many reasons. Here are a few of them:-

#MeToo

Nearly half a century of experience with one penis or another.

My re – evaluation of many of those experiences in light of age, wisdom and maturity, and a sad realisation of how many of them were abusive and exploitative, and how naïve I once was.

MY present situation of over 20 yrs of a deliciously happy heterosexual marriage that shows no sign of lessening any year soon.

My understanding of the vast gap between one sort of sexual encounter and another and how many people miss out on their potential for love, pleasure and deeply life enhancing relationships

My love of helping people live more fulfilled lives, and opening up debates – you may not agree and I can hear the voices of disagreement arising as I write, but do please give it some deeper consideration instead of being defensive about your current experiences and perceptions. These are not judgements but thought provoking suggestions.

My willingness to say things that others might not want to be seen or heard saying out loud (thank my ADHD and mindfulness / openness training for that).

My determination to support the really positive changes in sex and gender identity and equality for all across the whole planet (half of anything from this book will go to charities who already do that great work supporting trafficked women and children).

My sadness that so many women and men still undervalue or are even completely unaware of their inner, deeper, wonderful sexual selves and sell themselves short (the 'turkeys that vote for Christmas' syndrome).

My knowledge that I also still have much to learn; this book can become a conversation (well mannered of course), to continue this discussion for the benefit of all, and only in that direction.

My love of the spiritual journey of life and taking each day as a new adventure into becoming a kinder wiser person, whilst knowing that I still have much to learn myself, a joyful journey that never ends.

My wish that I had known this younger in life but then I wouldn't have had the experience base from which to write this.

Half of all proceeds from this book go to

Anti-Slavery International is the only UK-based charity exclusively working to eliminate all forms of slavery throughout the world by investigating and exposing current cases of slavery, campaigning for its eradication, supporting the initiatives of local organisations to secure the freedom of those in slavery or vulnerable to it, and pressing for more effective implementation of national and international laws against slavery. Founded in 1839 by British abolitionists, it is the world's oldest international human rights organisation.

Topics covered

Is there a penis in your life

Consent not coercion

The Penis / everything else relationship

Relationship with its resident male

The conjoining member

Names

    - What is the personality of the resident penis

    - How to name your penis

    - The naming ceremony

    - Negative name associations

    - Musical name options

Hormones

Hygiene and health

Learning to wait its turn

Politeness and consent

The shadowy, more sinister sides of the penis culture- the sex industry

Size

Boasting

Appropriateness

Pornography

Censorship and shame

Masturbation

First times

Female genital mutilation

Whoops ..... and there it goes!

Condom disasters

Responsibility

Rape and recovery

The psychology of the Penis

The Spiritual Penis

The penis at playtime.

Other playtimes

And Finally.......

The Well Mannered Penis

Is there a penis in your life?

What is the quality of your relationship with this penis?

Is it fun; was it once fun, do you want it to be a relationship that is fun?

Have you enjoyed relations with a penis or has it been a huge disappointment with which you can no longer be bothered?

Are you afraid of the penis in general either through direct experiences or through cultural portrayals and knowledge of power abuses to other people? After all there is enough about that in the media currently in one way or another.

Your immediate responses to these questions will tell you where you are right now and possibly if you want to repair or improve or just accept that is where it's at. That is your choice. This book is not meant to be a sex manual, nor a relationship guidance work; there are plenty of them out there already. Instead I want to open up this discussion about the penis and why it has become so unpopular in certain areas of life and how we can heal that for everyone's benefit.

How we relate to a penis can have an enormous effect on how happy we are and this can be in so many ways. I hope we can share some ideas which you can take on from here.

This is a time of revelation (to men) just roughly how many women feel they have been sexually abused or harassed, and to women just how much they have accepted that imbalance of power, even endorsed their own subordination and abuse. So it seemed a book by a woman on a well mannered penis should be offered up to the debate.

I think much of this would apply to anyone who is in a relationship with the owner of a penis, even if they have one them self.

Mostly we all want happy well balanced functional relationship – there are always exceptions of course, and they have their own books.

Whilst I cannot help but make this a tongue in cheek book, it also has some serious messages and points for contemplation. I am open to suggestions for further sections if they contribute to the overall message and are not excluding, or offensive, to anybody

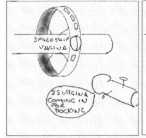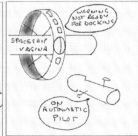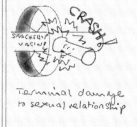

Consent – not coercion

All interactions with any penis must be fully and mutually consensual. To understand that, we must explore what is not consensual. The following are all wrong.

There must be no emotional blackmail – you owe me, if you really love me, you went with him so why not me, I really need this now even if you are not in the mood, if you say no I will tell everyone you are frigid, even if you say no I will tell everybody you said yes anyway.

There should be no expectation – you said yes last time so why not now, it is my right because you are my wife/partner.

No sense of threat or power play – I am your boss, I am physically stronger than you, I have money so can buy you, I have status so you should be grateful for my attentions, if you don't give me what I want I might not be responsible for the consequences.

No hint of bribery - I am older than you so can teach you things that someone your own age would never know about, if you have sex with me I will enhance your career, make you feel special, spend money on you, take you places to show off about. Of course women can do this too, so we all need to be aware of this one!

Exploitation of vulnerable people – is this person emotionally needy, lacks self confidence, comes from a troubled background, been institutionalised, recently abandoned or separated, facing hardship of some sort or another, is left with few other choices.

Penis fear – not everybody will have this but some do as a result of their negative life experiences, either directly through sexual abuse or through emotional abuse from Male members of their family circle. Being aware of this, just as a possibility, can be an important stage in developing a well mannered penis of your own. IF the point of this book is to lovingly heal the rifts in PTU/PDU relationships, we have to acknowledge the role fear will have.

No intoxication - you are drunk so I can take what I want, date rape drugs are self explanatory but self induced drugs are not and whoever may choose to experiment thus and trust in those around should be respected while they are intoxicated, as a duty of mutual care and self respect of those others.

Any Yes on any of these bases is not consent with any real meaning. They are effectively abusive and should be considered as rape or sexual assault. Even if the word yes or ok is heard, if it comes from this place then it is not consent as it should be. Once everyone in the world understands this, it will begin a revolution in improved relationship with the penis on all levels, for all parties.

The Penis / everything else relationship

The penis, in many if not all relationships, is the bridge between the emotional context and the physical. You cannot blame the penis for those parts for which it is not responsible. Neither can it make up for that which is lacking elsewhere. The penis is the penis, that is all it is and that is all it needs to be. But how it behaves, how well mannered it is depends on the ideology of its owner. The penis is part of many relationships, in many directions.

The well mannered penis is a happy chappie

Relationship with its resident male.

Each penis has a relationship with its penile transportation unit, the male (PTU), the PDU – penile docking unit - being its counterpart.

This penis / PTU relationship should be one of mutual respect and appreciation but it often is not. Factors which dilute or undermine a healthy man/ penis relationship may be to do with competition with other men and self image given to them by the media in one form or another. PDU (women's) expectations can greatly contribute to this but mostly it is up to the PTU to develop its own paradigm about its Penis. This brings us to the whole psychology thing – later.

Women who fall into this mindset may consider a man needs to be this or that, and usually ignore their masculine emotional needs completely. 'Men don't cry'. In my view the world would be a far nicer place if they were allowed to cry more often when feeling distressed. They expect men to be sensitive to their needs but men should perform! Well that is about as unkind as it gets and denies so much of our shared humanity. The penis is not a performer.

The well mannered penis
shouldn't worry about
performing

But this general 'commodity' attitude to any partner is a major flaw in our thinking. It undermines the quality of our relationships and fails to recognise the debt of gratitude we may have towards each other and especially towards this male member when it is at its best.

We are all people, humans and individuals, with all that that brings to a relationship. The penis is a wonderful but small part of that. The most wonderful thing we can offer a potential life partner is allowing them to be who they are in the deepest levels inside and out and that this whole person is utterly accepted and loved for all their attributes, flaws and greatnesses included.

Freedom to be who they are in their core means they can drop the big man act or the little woman act too. We can be equals, be empowered and joyfully embracing sexual activity as part of that self expression.

So it is ok, or should be, for men to show and need emotional connection during sex as it is for a woman. To cry even, with the beauty of that spiritual connection, of truly being loved, and free to enjoy that experience without any fear. That is when sex becomes the mystical union that is love and must not be confused with oxytocin, the sexually released neurotransmitter of deep contentment and wellbeing, but which wears off.

Very few women have that and sadly very few men have that either!

The 'macho' man expectations and projections and the 'girlie girl' paradigms of feminine beauty and womanhood prevent this very thing that we all most deeply crave, the deep heart, body and soul connection. The true connections we are all capable of but which have been written out of the modern human narrative and replaced by superficiality and artifice.

We may not even know that we crave that level of connection, and many are afraid of it due to childhood damage, but it is still there inside each of us and we all know that on a deeper level which is what drives us to create unions that are beyond procreation and mating/resources.

Some men find their relationship with their penis is one of disappointment or even self / member rejection. Except, you can't reject something that is an integral part of your body and for whom you are the transportation unit!

But for some men it is equated with status and thus they might think they are inadequate as humans based on the size and status of their penis. This is addressed in more detail later on but generally this is a huge misunderstanding of the role of the penis in your life.

Men - take note of this point. You are not your penis and your penis is not you, any more than your ear or hand is you. So your overall worth is not measured by the length or girth of your penis, it is to do with how you behave in yourself. Be the best you that you can manage and learn how to self reflect so that you can manage your own emotional development and maturity in all matters emotional and sexual.

Women take note too. You are not your body either and if you don't want to be treated like a piece of meat then return the compliment to the other part of your coupledom, whoever they may be.

The conjoining member

The penis is the organ of conjoining with the one being loved, the penile docking unit (PDU). Sometimes the Docking unit may also have a penis.

Well managed penis sometimes like other well manered penis.

That does not matter, the same rules should always apply.

This should be a joyful and wonderful part of the overall relationship and it often is the most focussed part of a relationship, especially in the early days when oxytocin is the drug of choice and the bonding effects of its influence are at their height.

This is when the foundations of a long lasting relationship are laid down, or the intensity of a shorter encounter, are also fully enjoyed. It is that release of oxytocin that makes us feel so high and in love and open and flowing free.

This however cannot last if the overall relationship is not fully developed and I believe that the relationship with the penis is a very important part of that development lasting happily and long into the future. Again this point is developed later on.

Names

Why name the penis in your life? Good question!
Here are some possible reasons: why not after all? It's
fun. It's a shared thing. You can have conversations
using the name , even in public and hope that no one
gets who it is you are talking about e.g. How is 'Fred'
feeling today oh he will need a massage later on for sure.

The penis is character in your relationship with its own special role, so why not make it personal to his character and so you both know who you are talking about, not a random penis but this very special one that you share.

A much-loved Penis should have its own name and personality in a relationship, so that it feels included and valued as the unique and carefully designed organ that facilitates those wonderful experiences of conjoining with the one you love. Seriously this can be a joyfully fun thing to play with between intimate couples.
The chosen name would be something that best describes it character, its personality, and its contribution to the relationship.

What is the personality of the relevant penis?

There are various possibilities, for instance how does it behave when resting? - Mr sleepy / snoozy

How quickly does it spring into action when required? - everyready or everard?

Does it poke and prod its PDU in the back when lying in spoons position when just resting or going to sleep, or even if it has just had its fun, more or less demanding further attention, or is it happy to rest in the loving afterglow?

Does it try to dominate conversation about other things? All these characteristics suggest pet names that could evolve. Each penis is an individual in so many ways. Does it mind being played with in the bath as a favourite shared bath time toy and not have to lead to full intercourse or arousal? More on that later.

Does it mind being sung to or with, the foreskin being very useful to make into a pretend singing mouth with lips? A penile ventriloquist partner, with which you can have endless fun making up voices for and mad cap conversations with such as 'How was your day?', - 'dark and sweaty', -' oh sorry to hear that, do you feel better now you are floating free in the bath?'. These conversations help to create a relaxed relationship with the penis that is less sexual predator and more fun playtime friend

Does it like to be greeted in the morning with a friendly little pat and a cuddle, or reassuringly and lovingly cupped and stroked at night before going to sleep? Just to say hello to or good night to. This reassures the insecure penis it is still loved and wanted any how it is and it doesn't always have to be on duty!

Is it happy to go to warm glows starting and to feeling stretchy and allow that to sink back again?

Can it enjoy all these intimate and loving playful activities without needing to develop into full sexual encounters every time?

The answers to these questions are also part of its place in the relationship with the penile docking unit (PDU) and thus the names it might suggest.

Nothing is right or wrong however and I must make that clear. The behaviour of the penis is what it is. It can be modified up to a point and age will also have a part to play in that characteristics list. But the most significant issues are how it plays its part in the consensual relationship it is a key part of, with the emphasis on consensual.

Many of them are also a reflection of the character of its PTU and a barometer of the level of playfulness and intimacy of the relationship the penis may find itself engaged in.

How to name your penis?

Well the naming should either be a joint thing or come from the partner. After all they are on the receiving end of it and thus know it well enough to understand its character and proclivities.

A good name can come out of that with some clarity and appropriateness. I cannot suggest names for you however, that must come from the people involved in the naming of that relationship, just like naming a newborn child must come from its parents.

The naming ceremony

This should be part of the creation of a truly intimate and loving relationship and can be celebrated in whatever way all think appropriate. A penis with a name will never feel left out of conversations or overlooked or undervalued and under-appreciated. After all they can be quite sensitive souls as well as being as horrifically insensitive as is possible. This relationship is one key dimension to an emotionally healthy and well-mannered penis. A suggestion though could be a sort of fun 'knighting' ceremony when the erect member is given its full name with honour and dignity, followed by a lot of fun.

Negative name associations.

The downside of naming a penis is often to be found in the names given to their members by some men. These have intrinsic messages in them which are not conducive to a well mannered penis. I loved frank Zappa's outrageous musical humour and I remember laughing at the claim that his dick was a Harley which you kicked to start. Well really I think most men would find that a tad painful. But that was possibly the point, unless it was the concept of 'a good ride' which might be seen as fun but could also be seen as derogatory and is certainly used thus against women. The penis was made out to sound like a weapon, a mighty thing, a member to be feared. So we can laugh and enjoy the release of tension that accompanies that laughter in difficult areas of life. But like humour there can be a dark side to this kind of name and the recipients of that dark side are not ever going to be laughing. Even though I cannot help the numerous puns scattered throughout this piece of writing, I am deeply aware of that dark side.

So I ask you, how on earth can a Harley become a loving, tender plaything?

Musical name options

Music comes up with many naming options such a ding a ling ling – by Chuck Berry, Diddy wah diddy sung by many but written originally by Blind Blake; also a version by Willie Dixon, himself sporting a male member pseudonym.

And who thought that My Boy Lollipop was really about Oral Sex in the 1960's, my parents certainly wouldn't have had a clue. 'Dust my broom' is another penile analogy in song along with 'squeeze my lemon' by Robert Johnson and then by Led Zeppelin, 'rattle snake shake' by Peter Green's Fleetwood Mac.

There are many more that you can think of here too I am sure, and we can chortle away at them happily.It is sadly however a deep influence on how some men view their members and it is possibly behind many of the misogynistic attitudes that men hold against women with their penis at its centre.

So let us look at the names given by men to their own penis. Dick, Todger, Cock, Tool. So far nothing kind or gentle there. I would not use Dick as the name as it suggests something also stupid.

Think of the connotations of the word dick, dickhead, right dick, all meaning stupid penis, stupid man. How can a Penis feel good about itself and thus be well mannered if is also feels bad about itself because of all this anatomical derision.

 So many names- so many connotations!

Be careful how you name your penis. It may have hidden consequences that are deeply detrimental to your relationship with this member.

Little boys learn early on through this naming that a penis is something to be used as a power weapon and yet is stupid and worthless and something that deserves to be both ashamed of and in the next moment brandished as a power tool might be, a sign of manhood.

These names create such deeply damaging paradigms around the penis that could be akin to racially and gender based inappropriate language.

Hormones

We like to think we are in control of our minds bodies and behaviours, but we so are not.

Once you start looking into the psychology of the brain / mind and body overlaps you realise that hormones play a huge and significant part in all our lives, and no less so with the well mannered penis and his best female friends.

Men have testosterone. This is what makes them men and not women.

When a foetus is developing in uterus it could be either gender in the first few weeks, but this is the hormone that specifies the final gender designation of the child born as going to be a man and thus a PTU, although in some cases it is less than clear.

Some men have more than others, hormones I mean.

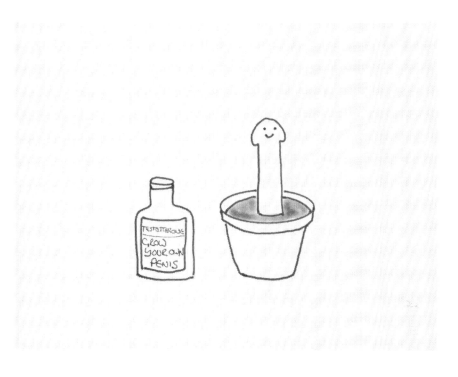

Most have them raging through their young male bodies during early adolescence and young adult lives, and then hopefully they calm down and give the resident PTU a bit more peace.

Women also have hormones although these are not usually commented on until they become a 'problem' through PMT, Menopause and pregnancy.

As both genders may have some difficulty in controlling their behaviour due to the influences of these hormones, it seems to me that the conversation about them needs to be out in the open, especially to boys who risk being turned into the PTU's of very badly behaved Penis.

Men and women alike can exhibit behaviour that would be described as 'not really them', but the male version can have devastating consequences for his bad behaviour and thus a well mannered penis makes sure he is fully understanding of both his own and everyone else's hormonal issues, and finds non-harmful methods to manage it.

Likewise docking units need to manage their own and inform themselves of male hormones and the influences they can exert on their transportation units.

The key to a well mannered penis and healthy male / female relationships is full and mutual appreciation of what the other experiences as well as your own.

It is not up to women to make allowances for men and then not have that same acceptance in return but it is not up to men to take advantage of their hormone arguments to blame women for their own sexual abuse.

A well mannered penis is always courteous of the 'other'.

Hygiene and health

A well mannered penis should always check that the recipient of its goodwill welcomes it as it is presented. Mostly, docking units would prefer that to be freshly washed and without the cheesy bits that collect under a foreskin or the smell of stale urine. Occasionally the natural fragrance of genitals can be part of the arousal and excitement of a sexual relationship so there is no prescriptive rule of thumb here but a well mannered penis would always check first and respect the preferences of its docking unit.

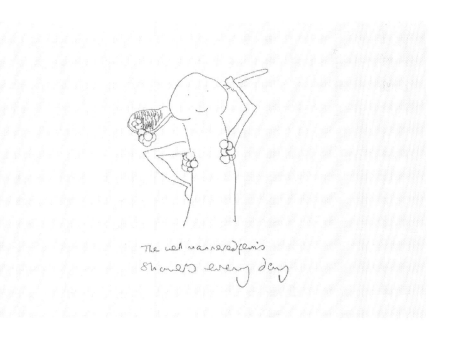

The well mannered penis
showers every day

We all want a healthy body and the penis is no exception. Infections that are minor but annoying, such as Thrush, can be caused by too much soap since this alters the natural PH from slightly acid to too alkaline. Gentle and occasional use of diluted vinegar can do no harm at all though and will protect both PDU and PTU from such infectious infestations.

Wearing a condom is obvious when necessary. I won't go into too much detail here other than to remind men that this protects themself and well as their partners from other nasties which have more serious connotations.

If you enjoy having sexual interactions then learn to love your penis enough to protect him from potentially devastating consequences, respect his need to health care. Would you knowingly go into a room of highly infectious people and not feel some concern for your own well-being?

Have the same concern for your marvellous member then please. That way you don't have to deal with the indignities of curing this nasty concerned, or learning to live with it since many are not curable nowadays!

If you want to enjoy a long and loving relationship with your penis then take good care of it and respect it as you would a new born child. After all it has the power to reward you richly through your whole life if you take good care of it at all times.

The well mannered penis never minds donning outdoor wear

Circumcision is also a topic under hygiene since this was the original purpose of the removal of the cowl which protects the penis head from too much friction when flaccid.

Otherwise known as the foreskin, it has a design function, but sometimes it is removed for various reasons, including because it is too tight to work properly and will cause discomfort instead of reducing it. However it is often removed as part of initiation rites and sometimes this might be male genital mutilation since a baby or child can rarely give informed consent, and even an adolescent might be made to feel obliged because of custom or tradition, just as so many girls are forced to endure unspeakable and life- ruining mutilation to their genital area.

I consider this an area of deep controversy but one that needs further exploration.

Tradition, custom, culture, all these words are up for challenge while we explore how to develop true equality between the sexes and gender identity options.

Learning to wait its turn

This is basically good manners and is applied according to the relationship each penis finds itself engaged in, thus there can be no hard and fast rules (sorry can't help it), and the pornographers idea of hard and fast sex is not always what every ordinary recipient actually wants. Many years ago the Pointer Sisters released a wonderfully sexy song called 'Slow hand'.

For those of you who are musically orientated this is also a cool name for a cool guitarist called Eric Clapton. But back to the Pointer Sisters, they want a slow hand and an easy touch, someone who is willing to spend some time, not come and go in a heated rush.

Now strictly speaking this is not all down to the penis but it can play a huge part in this.

The skin on the head of a penis is beautifully soft and is wonderful when rubbed gently against a woman's equally soft and delicate parts of exquisite pleasure. Sadly this is not possible if its owner is convinced that all that is needed is lots of thrusting and grunting, in most cases at least.

We all have moments when we feel some urgency and need for rampant sex but often this does not work in orgasmic terms for women.

There are many women who never really enjoy sex because this is how it is conducted, thus they can never become happily friends with their resident penis.

I cannot speak for male partners here.

Thinking back to the naming section and the implications of these choices, the penis is preferably not viewed as a weapon or a machine; it is a beautiful organ capable of giving much deeply loving shared pleasure. Which leads us onto....

Politeness and consent

Consent is crucial here and that is the first point to make. It is very impolite to force a penis onto (through self-exposure alone), or into someone's orifice who does not want it, at that moment or ever. Full consent must be abundantly clear each and every time. I am amazed and astonished that this is such a controversial issue. It really should not be at all, but it is, so I shall continue to explore this issue here too.

Can no ever really mean yes?

Probably not since even yes does not always mean yes. Sometimes people say yes because they are too afraid to say no, or they say no tentatively because they are afraid to stand up for themselves.

It is impolite of the penis to continue at this point and there are ways of coping with the male modular brain which when in full sexual drive mode can seem to be beyond any ability to reason at all.

In large part the point of developing a healthy relationship with the penis in your life is to prevent these issues continuing.

The playful fun relationship can make it easier to manage the dominant urgency that some men feel, or the need to feel empowered by sexual activity when it is the power that needs to be addressed not the sexual urges.

The shadowy, more sinister sides of the penis culture- the sex industry

There is a whole section of society across the world who have been left emotionally damaged by a childhood where they were not allowed to say no appropriately, where they were not taught good safe boundaries, where they were not taught now to value their own physical or psychosexual wellbeing and integrity.

Although they may say yes and even defend their right to say yes, what they most want is connection, to be valued, given affection, approval, attention even. Just some smidgeon of something that they can cling onto, and sex can so easily be confused with love because of all those neurotransmitters, when it is just not there at all. These are the people who are vulnerable to being trafficked or manoeuvred into the sex industry in so many ways, to act in porn films, to be prostitutes or call girls, escorts, striptease and sex shows. Boyfriending is a common tactic using exactly these vulnerabilities but treating the individual and a commodity to be groomed for exploitation.

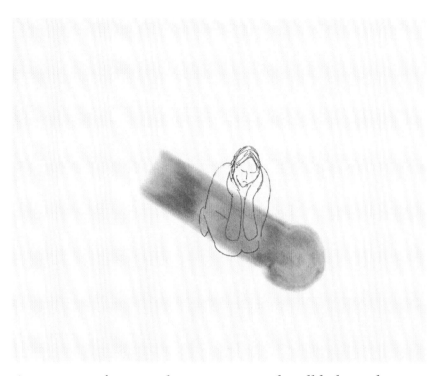

A very, very few people are strong and well balanced who go into these industries with the intention of exploiting the punters. They do exist though. But might even they unintentionally be inciting someone else to act in an abusive way towards someone who is not consenting. We might never know but it could be worth a consideration.

Politeness during consensual partnered sexual activity

A well mannered Penis is always polite. It waits its turn to do its own thing because many, many clitori need more time and different activities to entice that sometimes elusive orgasm out of them.

What a penis needs to understand is that the most fun is not always the booster thrust, approach. First of all it needs to relax about itself and its own needs.

Then it can explore ways to play with itself and its partner in non-thrusty ways to start with.

I don't need to be explicit here since a well mannered penis will want to explore this for itself anyway and a little imagination can work wonders.

Most PDU's can also take part in this exploration and make it part of the fun of the relationship. Sex is not and should never be something either party 'DO' to the other. It is best when it is a shared, fun, exploration of bodies and what they can achieve together.

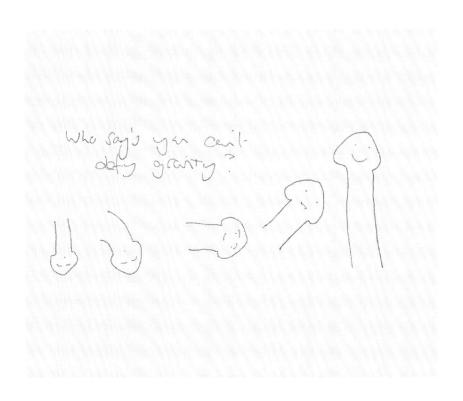

So a well mannered penis can wait. It can inflate and deflate a little perhaps while it is in waiting and anticipation and then return to its former glory when its moment has arrived naturally and without shame or embarrassment.

A well-mannered, confident, and happy penis can do all this and still get all the fun it can possibly need.

Size

Size is often far too important for many PTU's than it should be, and gets translated into worthiness, manliness and sexual attractiveness. It represents none of these things. But let us face it Guys, the penis changes shape and size all the time anyway, doesn't it, from almost disappearing when in cold water i.e. the sea, to the enlarged organ of what should be loving tenderness.

The well mannered penis
Comes in all shapes and sizes

And then there are showers and growers. I mean as in those who show all they have and more or less stay the same but firmer, and those whose proportions change greatly on full inflation.

The latter are a lot of fun to play with, but both are great, and neither should be a source of shame or anxiety.

Incidentally the same is true here of female labia. What you have right now is just great and all you need if you approach it open-mindedly and open heartedly too.

Size is not that important for most PDU's.

The overall relationship is what matters. However there are some misconceptions that perhaps it would be good to allay here.

The penis comes in all shapes and sizes.

No news there.

But some men don't seem to realise the same is true for vaginas too, or whichever orifice is your orifice of preference.

But for the purpose of this paragraph I shall mostly be focussing on the vagina.

Sadly some women also perpetuate this myth and are themselves encouraged to believe that size matters far more than it needs to.

Love, connection, and a sensitive, open, playful, deeply connected sexual relationship, are far more important than size in anything.

Thus we have to challenge these accepted norms as not acceptable for true equality, for either party.

The genitalia you have are fine however you are endowed, male or female, you just have to find the partner for whom this match also works.

When the well manered penis
finds a good friend he is
truly happy

The vagina is the gateway to the whole amazing delicate reproductive system for a woman and it includes the neck of the cervix.

This is a sensitive part of a woman's anatomy and needs to be treated with respect. An oversized penis that bashes its head against the cervical neck will not be much fun for the PDU, in fact is it likely to cause sensations that are more akin to period pains than anything pleasurable.

So the right sized penis for each vagina is what is needed, unless you have had a hysterectomy. If that is not so easy, then finding accommodating positions is the next best option, and again requires careful exploration for both parties.

There is probably the right penis for every vagina and the right position for every couple. Part of the fun of exploration.

Some cervix necks hang down further than others and this also varies at different times of the month and according to other activities that naturally occur in the lower abdomen. Some are placed further back or higher up.

Every vagina and clitoris is different and understanding that is an important thing for a well mannered penis to take into consideration when priding itself on its proportions.

It may feel impressive to its owner but it may be a source of great discomfort to the PDU and thus not conducive to a loving healthy relationship.

Although the vagina is capable of stretching to accommodate a child's head being born, this is generally acknowledged as being very painful.

Sexual relationships are meant to be a pleasurable experience and thus anything that might cause pain to a woman will instantly negate that pleasure.

So if you are overly endowed please also be courteous about your partners accommodation needs and allow them time to open sufficiently to meet your needs too.

In fact always be considerate in this way no matter your size and enthusiasm, know the right time to 'do your thing' and when to wait.

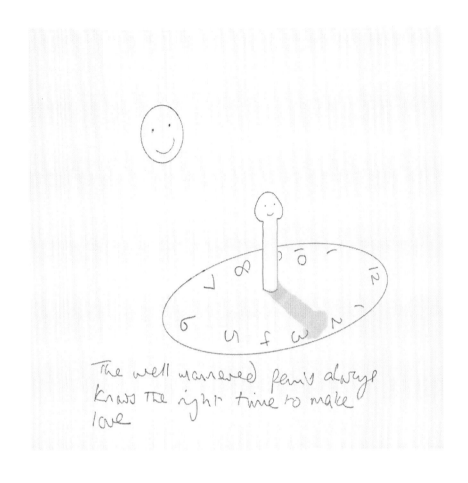

The well mannered penis always knows the right time to make love

The vagina is a truly amazing and resilient part of a woman's anatomy but it needs treating with deep respect to get the best from it and to give it encouragement to want this to continue. Violent sexual experiences can also leave it too damaged to fulfill its other function which is to grow and deliver a baby. This leads me onto the next topic

Boasting

A Catholic priest is working in the confessional. A man comes in and says "Father - I'm 82 years old and last night I had sex with two 24 year-old girls. Twice!"

The priest replies "Well, my son, you need to say a dozen Hail Marys for your contrition."

"But Father, I'm not Catholic" replied the old man.

"Well, then why are you telling me this in confession?"

"Father - I'm 82 years old. I'm telling *everybody*!"

What is wrong with this joke? Yes it made me laugh but then I thought – what if I was one of those girls and someone was boasting about 'having' me like this. It might hurt like hell. It might make that woman feel used, junk, and worthless. It might, in extreme circumstances unknown to this 82 yr old man, leave the young woman concerned feeling suicidal.

It is not the sex that is the problem, it is the abuse of power as an afterword, boasting about how you had sex with someone immediately strips it of its sanctity, its connectedness, its respect of someone else.

This tendency towards treating PDU's as commodities starts in young male hood when boys are beginning to turn into young men but lack the emotional maturity or 'sense of other' and their potential emotional vulnerability sufficiently to behave well.

We can to a certain limit allow boys to be boys, although we do need to educate them quickly at this stage, before this kind of attitude becomes entrenched too deeply.

But when men still haven't grown up and started considering their responsibility to others, then it is extremely ill-mannered of them, and no matter how old you are, inexcusable to boast like this to 'everybody'.

Lovely – you had great consensual sex, enjoy it quietly inside yourself and respect the sanctity of that conjoining. What you don't boast about makes you a far bigger person – man- than telling everyone what you did have.
How sad that at 82 you still feel the need to boast and are not in a loving relationship that continues to have a loving sexual context but if not then don't abuse young women to make your own ego bigger.

That is the other way of looking at that joke, and far more realistic.

And the same applies to women. Men have feelings too although not always in the same way.

Pornography

This is an interesting issue. Why is Porn such a hot topic anyway? I know some people do use it together in loving relationships and as long as they can be utterly certain that there was no exploitation in the making of that imagery, it is doing no harm to others.

And of course fictional written porn can be nothing but a non-abusive choice, as long as it is not inflicted coercively to act out onto unwilling others.

But it brings up some other questions for my curious mind, which I would like my readers to also consider in some depth.

Why might some men want to visually watch other men, with usually oversized members that would actually have many women running for cover, have sex with a woman who is probably, almost certainly, faking it?

It is an interesting point to ponder on in the relationship with the penis overall for both men and women. I mean, it would possibly make more sense for men to want to watch lesbian porn only.

OR are they imagining they are this super stud they are watching and that is fulfilling their fantasy for how they want to think they should be having sex.

Vicarious sex may not do much for your real sexual relationship though, because of that word relationship, there is none in porn, it is all acting of a sorts, for money and some sort of fame or recognition of sorts that has little to do with self esteem and self worth and a lot to do with self harm. You might be proud of your body but pride is not self worth.

SO porn is acting, rarely particularly good acting.

And that is what it is, a fantasy which is exploiting everyone concerned in one way or another, even though they might not think or realise they are being exploited, they are because no one is a commodity.

A human is a person, a living breathing human personality and thus not a commodity to be used in this way.

Pornography just increases the emotional isolation of sex from love and turns it into a cheap thrill more appropriate for sweaty horny kids just finding and fulfilling their sexual urges rather than an adult having a full sexual relationship.

If you use it to spice up your waning sex life, then perhaps try to find non exploitative ways to do this for your own sake.

Literature probably harms fewer people that films or photos. Or you might want to achieve this by developing this special relationship in ways that will be lasting into old age. Many people do achieve this well, so why not you too?

I can hear the justifications for why pornography is acceptable and load s of people do it, but can you be sure absolutely certain that there was no exploitation in any way in the making of that film.

If you thought a child was being treated as a slave to bring you your daily hot chocolate would you say that acceptable, so arguably porn is the same thing.

Just be informed and willing to go beyond your current model of thinking, expand it out to the inter connectedness of everything in life and how unintentionally you may be contributing to the sexploitation of someone else who is not in a position to say 'no'.

This is not a moralising point but an invitation to go beyond your personal sense of consumers rights and needs to consider what is behind that, and to rethink the need for external titillation.

Why not find the real spiritual sexual connection that takes you to far greater levels of emotional expression and pleasurable ecstasy.

A well mannered penis will be far happier if this approach is taken and it can also find ways to express itself openly and without performance fear.

The sex industry is huge and worth a lot of money, so if it is taking your money, you may like to consider - are you also being exploited?

The complexities of this topic would take up an entire book on its own (and not one I want to write either) so I am just hoping to provoke a little alternative perspective here. The debate should be opened up to all perspectives to make sure that no-one and nothing is leading to abuse a little further down the line, we are all responsible for this as a global community.

Appropriateness

A lovely Meme going round face book recently stated quite simply – *Your Granddad used to write your Grandma love letters longer than a college thesis. Now here you are texting women pictures of your penis*
By Rebel Circus

YOU can do better than that I am sure!

No dick pics. SIMPLE. Not unless they are specifically requested and even then I would be wary – never forget revenge porn is a thing against men too.
Nothing much more to say here except the penis belonging to the man you love can be a joyously beautiful thing to behold, and play with, in context.
The penis of David skilfully carved by Michelangelo is also a wondrous beautiful thing, as are the many male naked images in art. But any other sticky sweaty hairy penis is just not what most docking units want to see out of context.

Perhaps freshly from the shower might be less worrisome. We can all be a bit sweaty and smelly at times and to our own beloved that might even be attractive but not to the unknown ' other'.

It is all a matter of appropriateness. It is never appropriate to send to someone who has not expressed a desire for such an image to be sent to them

A penis holds its beauty in context to the whole man, indeed the genitals of the one you love may be quite enchanting.

Yet of itself neither the vagina nor the penis are innately attractive, and both need to be viewed as part of the whole rather than a piece of anatomy from which to extract sexual pleasure.

A man is more than his penis and a woman is more than her vagina, to see anything less than the whole person is deeply inappropriate.

I love my PTU's body and have certain favourite parts which I find particularly attractive TO ME, but only ever in context of the whole wonderful man that he is and has been for the last 20+ years

Women mostly don't want to know about your penis specifically if they are not emotionally and sexually partnered with you, even if they want to know about you as a person, a friend, a colleague, an acquaintance or neighbour.

Conjoined bodies can make visual knowledge of each other's genitals more intimate and delightful. Certainly better than the Victorian all under the nightgown and bed clothes and heaven help us if you see each other naked.

But only if you are the PTU who happens to be the beloved in their life.

The same applies to real life situations where some men like to just unzip and expose themselves to anyone they can obtain as a captive audience, especially when incorporated into a power imbalance in that relationship i.e. colleagues / subordinates.

As we know from the media outings of Weinstein, Louis CK and others, this is mostly to beautiful and aspiring women (and some younger men as with Kevin Spacey) who are in an unequal power relationship.

The PTU here could have been a wonderful mentor, nurturing the other's perceived talents and ambitions, but instead choose to use and abuse both the other and their own position, as we see ultimately bringing about their own undoing.

Some get away with it until death, like Jimmy Saville, but rarely is it never eventually public knowledge, and hopefully it will always be 'outed' immediately from now on. Too many male privilege assumptions is not a good thing for anybody

Censorship and shame

Two questions.

What do the Victorians and the Vatican have in common?

Why are there so many penis's in the Vatican vaults?

Answers to both are that they went around chopping them off statues because they didn't want to offend us delicate women, or incite other men into lustful thoughts about other PTU's.

Although we may laugh somewhat at this insanely and ridiculously naive and patriarchal attitude to women's sensibilities, I believe that the attitude has left some deeper seated mis-understandings about the penis for both men and women.

The Vatican excludes us women so it appears to be men worried about other men seeing the penis that led them to remove them all.

Perhaps they already knew about the sexual abuse of the younger men in their care and thought this might help the problem to go away.

Who knows how people of the past thought, but what we do know is that their attitudes have done the penis and its PTU no good at all and this is what we all need to address, for the sakes of both PTU and PDU.

The Vatican art collection is one of the most amazing collections in the world and they have over a hundred thousand items, all beautifully preserved, since it has never really been under threat like so many other cities and heritage sites around the world.

All the penis images or representations were chopped off and / or covered by fig leaves by the order of Pope Pius IX. Some of his successors also continued with this tradition.

Supposedly there is no statue with a visible penis in Vatican today.

So, where did they all go?

There is a room somewhere in the Vatican museum
vaults with all those penises carefully wrapped and
preserved, stored in wooden boxes. There is currently an
ongoing debate about restoring these penile pieces of art
to their original state. Perhaps one day you can visit the
Vatican and view the historical account of the penis
through art. But currently they are either removed or
covered.

AS far as I know the Victorians were less thoughtful and there are now many many statues whose removed appendages are lost forever, broken into rubble.

Imagine the time spent lovingly carving each stone penis and think of how these attitudes to this piece of anatomy have destroyed its good name.

The Penis in general is not a particularly pretty appendage, unlike say a buttock or shoulder.

But to the lover of a particular penis, when fully appreciated, it is a thing of attractiveness, wonder and joy, even beauty.

This is what we are being shown in a well carved penis.

A harmless stone penis can be a thing of beauty and thus we are introduced to the notion of a well mannered penis through art.

Masturbation

Punishing the act of masturbation can probably be documented to the Roman Empire. As a largely matriarchal society, the Roman view of male masturbation was as an unwelcome, undesirable act that directly affected procreation.

They needed more Romans so no wasting that precious seed please.

I don't think they understood how much seed was in one spoonful though.

More than they would ever need, thus we understand this attitude is borne out of ignorance, and this attitude based on ignorance has continued until today.

Christianity picked up this baton during the first century AD, defining the act as a 'Mortal Sin' and the spread of Christianity brought with it the crazy belief that self-abuse should be strongly discouraged in a Christian household.

Even today the Catholic Church still categorises masturbation as self-abuse, and as a 'venal and mortal sin', based on the same view, that the seed being wasted is precious and should only be used for procreation.

That this view limits and distorts the true nature of sexual experience as a joyful shared dimension of loving relationships is thus utterly smothered and lost in this shame and damnation attitude and I believe has also done much to create the negative views that both men and women have towards a penis.

As Steve Coogan, in character as Martin Sixsmith, in the film Philomena, says so simply and out of his irritation that a "loving God" might create something so pleasurable, then punish people if they don't abstain from enjoying it."

I agree with this viewpoint and think it is fundamentally mistaken, both in self-pleasuring and couple-dom. It is an unkind attitude to view sexual activity as wrong in any way at all, except if it is abusive and coercive or unwanted by one party.

It is an attitude that is deeply connected to and possibly behind so much of the damage around sexual activity because it has placed it into a limited category of permissions, and outside this an activity of shame and deserving punishment.

How does that distortion not put in into a unique position of both act of love and act of abuse and warfare against other people.

Masturbation can be a healthy thing. It can be the means to how you learn to manage your excitement, how to release pent up sexual energy without inflicting suffering on other people through rape or forced sexual behaviour and predation.

For goodness sake masturbation is fine done in private and hygienically dealt with. However masturbation in public places, in front of women who are not wanting this to happen and generally masturbating in public is not how a well mannered penis should go about its playtime.

If you want to get your penis appreciated then you have got to understand the psychology of the PDU/ PTU relationship.

Using masturbation as a form of sexual predation has been commented and reported in great detail recently in the press.

Harvey Weinstein, being the mostly widely and publicly denounced sexual deviant in this way. 'NO Harvey!' or anyone thinking of copying him.

Not in plant pots or onto women's bodies as an act of degradation and power 'because you can'. That is not ok and is decidedly badly mannered penis behaviour.

This will not lead to happy relationships with happy people and it will not lead to a contented penis with a fulfilled sex life.

Apparently though a few women who got mad with Weinstein came out to find him in tears, thus showing his damaged inner child abusing sexual power to feel empowered generally.

If those being abused can find their inner strength to know these truths, they may be able to fight back more effectively, but in reality no one should ever have to even think they should be in a position to do that

First times

The first time you actually have sexual intercourse, or any kind of sexual encounter, can be nerve wracking for both people concerned, whichever you are PDU or PTU. For everyone it is a huge and scary thing that we want to appear confident and experienced in – well most people do.

So let me start with female docking units. For most of them it just plain hurts. The penis is going into uncharted territory and it needs to open up. So consider this for a moment. Do you want to be remembered lovingly or with horror and regret.

It should matter to you if you are a well mannered penis at all. NO matter how much bravado you build up as a male PTU, treating a docking unit with anything less than tenderness is going to come back on you too one way or another.

So be kind be gentle talk to each other and don't have too many judgements or expectations. Remember what I said about Porn?

Do you want a genuine experience or one that is just plain dishonesty on all sides?

This book is not going to say what is ok and what is not, we are all individuals with our own preferences, but kindness in sexual expression is the most important thing to building intimacy that will last.

Your first may not be your last of course but it is the beginning of your sex life in general and I think most people want to remember it with happiness or at least not with confusion shame or unhappiness.

Female genital mutilation

This is a practice of cutting away many of the sensation creating areas of a woman's sexual anatomy for traditional and cultural reasons. The justification is that it prevents women being unfaithful. I shall not pass moral judgement on this as I am attempting to be as neutral as possible throughout this book.

 What I will say is this.

Men miss out so much by treating women like this. They lose the sensuous pleasure of being with a sexually liberated and aroused women who wants them and is enjoying herself as much as you are.

Men are missing out on a relationship based on equality of love commitment and shared adventure into the great exploration of what a sexual relationship can be in its entirety.

You are creating mutilated girls and women who can never really enjoy your sexual interactions with them because it will mostly be painful and debilitating for her. You are risking damaging her anatomically for the whole of her future, making her possibly incontinent, possibly unable to ever bear children.

DO I have to say much more than this to point out that a well mannered penis would not want this for their wives or their daughters. That women do it to each other is simply a manifestation of the demands that the PTU has placed on them in the past and can be educated out too.

Whoops ..... and there it goes!

 Premature ejaculation can be a bugbear for many men, and can disappoint many women. I am not expert n this but it seems to me from in most cases it is an over exaggerated sense of self and an insecure one at that, and this is what makes it go too fast. Too much desire to perform, control, be the best. Too much anxiety about being good enough, man enough, big enough even. All these have been addressed elsewhere and will in most cases greatly help a PTU overcome the too fast ejaculation.

All may not be lost though. IN youth this is more likely to happen because the younger PTU is rather spring loaded with hormones and thus a penis that cannot keep itself under control. Erections occur at the most inopportune moments and normal life can be difficult. So actually having an opportunity to explore with a willing and enthusiastic docking unit up to which ever stage is agreed upon, ca make it all too exciting to last for long. But a spring-loaded penis can usually recover quickly and continue soon afterwards.

Just give it time- use that time well to explore what a docking unit really likes and what they need time to think about. Find pleasure in being with someone in such an intimate context. Make sure you penis is a genial genital that is willing to accept its own limitations and can regroup a short time later on, ready to stay the course a little longer. And if it can't then no worries here either, just use other parts of your anatomy to make sure you give full and agreed satisfaction of encounter to your partner.

Condom disasters

These things happen.

Some condoms do not suit some men and can cause them to deflate.

Try different ones if this happens to you and do not be put off by it.

Remember the section of health and hygiene and do not let embarrassment put you at far greater risk of far greater embarrassment later on, with unwanted babies being made or unwanted infections

Sometimes they split – but normally they do not – so do check use by dates if you can make them last that long!

Be wary of long finger nails

Responsibility

If you have sexual activity you have to take responsibility for that activity and whatever it brings with it. For you and for each other!

I have mentioned health and hygiene and STD elsewhere but the other really important thing is what sexual intercourse is designed for.

Making Babies.

Pregnancy – it is you who puts the seed into its soil to grow babies with and that is a simple fact that you should never forget.

And to anybody else who might be implicated if you get this wrong.

There are too many unwanted and inadequately cared for children in this world. Don't add to their numbers. You are potentially ruining several lives and no matter how much you want to deny it, you are also responsible for putting the seed into places where babies grow.

Don't get me wrong, children are a wonderful gift. I adore my sons and grandson, but they are huge responsibility and for some people that is just too much.

Rape and recovery

If you commit rape you can be sure you have just possibly damaged someone's whole rest of their life. Most rapes are with someone known to the victim. So if this you remember that you have almost certainly broken their trust, and maybe not just with you if you knew them, but with all future relationships. You may have damaged them internally as they would not have been ready for you. You cannot make good on this ever, once committed this is it.

YOU cannot undo what you have done. So a well mannered penis will bear all this in mind and will never commit this act on anybody else ever.

The younger you understand this, the more likely you are to remember it and not become a badly behaved penis instead, and you will not be subjected to #MeTo campaigns or legal charges or public shaming. Every PTU needs to understand that rape is not in your best interests either.

If you are or have been raped you can remember a few things to help you get through.

Being raped is not who you are and not about you.

It is something horrendous that happened to you, shocking traumatising and just plain horrendous but it just happened to you, it is not who you are and it is not a judgement of you either.

It tells you a lot about the person who did this to you, about their level of emotional maturity and self respect, about their honesty and integrity, and probably about their childhood and emotional history and background.

Hopefully this book , small though it is , has enough punches packed into its words to make this issue become more understood and less likely to happen but if it has happened to you do not feel ashamed of it, do not let it destroy the beautiful person you are inside ,that we all are inside each of us.

No matter how badly behaved we are on the outside we all have that potential beauty inside us, but we don't always let it out.

The rapist is someone whose inner beauty is so deeply buried that they may never find it is there.

Don't let that happen to you too if you are raped. Don't be a victim, live your life with courage and bravery and move on. Don't ever let anybody tell you that it is your fault or you should have done more to protect yourself. Everyone has choices and there are always alternatives. Live well and learn to be happy again, and don't lose your ability to love life or others. Don't lose yourself to their darkness.

The Psychology of the Penis.

Here we can enter into the world of evolution and emotional literacy with a light touch because it is a weighty subject area, open to endless debates.

A penis has feelings but first and foremost it is designed to want sex, along with its PTU.

Procreation is the urge to pass on one's genes to a new generation of human, in other words to make babies, as many as possible, to populate the planet with humans. Well we have achieved that, possibly we humans are serious over achievers on that score, so that is no longer a necessity.

But the biological urge is primeval and has not gone away just because our goal had been reached globally. The individual penis does not generally know that the planet has enough people on it to last a long time and that we are in fact becoming a rash that the planet is struggling to heal itself from.

As I said this is a huge debate so I shall précis it right down.

The psychology of sex is a biological urge which creates a strong link between PTU and PDU. The end result pleasure of that urge is designed to ensure we want to do it and often, especially when in our prime, as it were, for potency of procreative powers.

On top of that we have the oxytocin effect which makes us want to bond with the sexual partner with the idea of raising those offspring to maturity.

As humans we also have a biological attachment to community/ tribe/ family connections because that is how we survive, collectively not individually.

We cannot make it alone, we are too vulnerable and weak, but collectively we are much stronger and more wily and clever and likely to thrive.

Bonding and love is the third dimension of this dynamic.

For some people this third dimension has become detached from the first two, the urges and the pleasure factors, and this detachment degrades the sexual expression from one of joyful union and harmony into one of abuse, self loathing and shame and many other things that could be listed here.

A well mannered penis does not need to feel these things, but for it not to, we must address the psychology of the 'game' of matching a PTU with a PDU.

Here is a range of quagmires and nightmares of fear and power games that we have already touched on elsewhere and which we all need to explore and understand before we can truly raise the penis from a place of denigration or abuse to the place which is deserves.

The penis should be a fully respected integrated member of society – but no more than the vagina which is utterly awesome in what it can achieve on behalf of the human race – think of it.

Men have huge power over women because they are generally bigger and stronger and can force a women to submit to sexual predation if they so choose

Women have huge power over men and their primeval urges to pursue mates and ejaculate into them for the good of the future of the population or their own immediate pleasure

Both sides can and do regularly abuse this power.

Both sides must learn to take responsibility not just for their own choices but for the ripple effect that those choices make for others in their gender group.

Women must not use the sexual attractiveness to gain power over men for the resources they might provide any more than men must not use their physical strength for gaining the gratification of a sexual release.

Love is not about, and should never be about power. Women should not use their power any more than men should use their power.

The penis wants to be wanted and loved just as much as its transportation unit does too.

Without love, the sexual act is generally distorted and debased into a self indulgence that is vulnerable to these negative emotions of guilt shame and self loathing and from there into revenge justification and abuse.

So women who use sex to 'win' an alpha male, just to possibly reject him for fun, are just as responsible for all those times when women are unable to say no and are not listened to by the penises who force themselves onto those women, or in some cases men too of course.

Flirting can be cruel and should not be used in this way in case those involved take it out on someone else another time. We might all be responsible indirectly for this.

Both parties must be saying yes, loud and clear, and in full understanding of what they are agreeing to and must have their emotional needs respected by the other parties.

Both partners! In any sexual act.

Anything else is placing that same act into a category it does not deserve, denigrated into a less that magnificent gift that we have been given though our bodies and it smacks of low self respect and low respect for the 'other'. The ripple effect of each individual's behaviour is the most important thing to understand. Women say that they have the right to dress and flaunt themselves as much as they want and it is only men who should use self restraint in this dance of sexual power.

As a feminist I am asking is that fair?

Should we also not take responsibility for our half of that game?

Making the best of ourselves is not about sexuality for one reason alone. Our sexuality is not the only thing that is best about us.

THE nicest kindest men I know are also deeply emotional creatures, but society does not take that into account in its images of masculinity any more than it does about women.

No one is a sexual of objective desire. We are all fully humans with emotions and needs and fears and skills and wonderful qualities.

A mindset that commodifies anybody is one of denigration and power.

This includes political and patriarchal ideologies as much as it does anything else.

If a human is viewed by the state as a unit of productivity then their basic humanity is being denied. But that is what happens and that is what our education system is all about, our political system, and employment /financial systems too. This all has its influence on how we view each other and each other's body parts, thus is part of the interconnected root of all sexual abuse.

 I don't want to go too deeply into debate about these ideas here. Just to highlight that it is all part of a mindset which leads to so many badly behaved penis and PTU's, and should therefore be a huge part of that discussion

The Spiritual Penis

In many parts of the planet the sexual organs have been elevated into spiritual subjects of veneration.

In some places genitals are given their own names and also sometimes separated from the rest of the body for significance. This practice comes from a more innocent time when body parts were not filled with notions of shame and revulsion. Thus one name for the penis is lingum, yoni being the female counterpart, docking area if you like.

These are nicer kinder names than those often given in western society and shows some of this understanding of the deeper importance of our relationship with these organs of procreation and relationship building

It is taken seriously in some Hindu practices and also tantric sex.

The sex act is seen as something leading to a form of enlightenment, presumably due to the bliss feelings it can induce, easily mistaken for spiritual bliss but really not the same thing at all, from experience.

That is the production of oxytocin, a feel good pleasure neurotransmitter designed to make us want to repeat the experiences so that we ensure a continuation of the species.

There is a museum dedicated to the Cham religion in southern Vietnam. This religion is closely related to Hinduism and the museum is filled with sculptures of linga everywhere.

There is one altar which had a central lingum surrounded by a circle of breasts as a sacred reminder of the importance of procreation.

Girls in this religion were protected closely until they came of marriageable age when there was a ceremony – after they had finished growing – that meant they were now available for courtship and marriage.

The feminine was respected but controlled by this custom. However a different view f both lingum and female which shows that change of attitudes can come about if enough people consider deeply their beliefs and assumptions about the sexual activities of the penis and its role in the lives of both PDU's and PTU's

Exploring this spiritual dimension of the penis can shed some light onto alternative ways of understanding its role in life.

But even this more spiritual practice became abusive in some cultures, with women brought into temples more or less as prostitutes of the priests, and perhaps it is the crossing over of patriarchal paradigms and sexual veneration that has led to the current situation where many women feel utterly objectified in general, even if not perhaps in their own hetero – relationships.

Again there is much to discuss and learn here.

As an aside, tantric sex is based on slow meditative activity, with the energy being built very intensely and gradually, so that the experience of climax can almost be an 'out of body' experience, sometimes spontaneously releasing kundalini energy, but certainly a whole lot deeper than a fuck following the use of e.g. porn. Whole course are available and whole books are written just on these topics. I simply want to introduce as many ideas about our friend the Penis as I am able in this project, so that we can understand him more and thus support him in his quest to become a well mannered penis.

Take your own exploration further and see where it leads
you in wonderful ways.

The psychology of the penis is after all mostly a
development of the spiritual approach to life; the word
psychology means study of the soul.

Even an already well-mannered penis might have more
to learn for its own complex system of beliefs and
enjoyment

The penis at playtime.

A well mannered penis needs some humility in its life and I wanted to end on a light note.

I am not so sure that everyone would think of this although I am sure many have, BUT - the penis has more than two purposes, excretion and reproductive/ sexual pleasure. It is also great fun to play with non- sexually, as many young boys find out for their own amusement, but as adults, PDU's can find this out too.

For instance, at shared bath time, a penis has a lovely tendency to float and bob around.

Shared baths can be great fun if the bath is big enough, but even when solitary bathing, your lover can come and play games with the bath toys, namely your penis. Just some examples could include:

- dancing the helmet around in the water pretending it is a mushroom in a Disney scene, humming appropriate background music
- using the foreskin to make lips that can sing any song you might like to sing karaoke to
- arranging bubbles from bubble bath on the head to see how many you can get on it in one go

The well mannered penis
can be fun in the bath

- seeing how long you can play with it before it starts
to inflate, and so on.

The penis can get very small when it first gets into the bath water, and then you can have fun watching it relax and celebrate its flexibility of shape and size.

Who can be afraid of a harmless lovely bath toy, or 'whatever time of day' activity toy you decide, without it having to go to sex all the time?

Other playtimes and games

Early morning wake-up games can include raspberry blowing and kissing with an affectionate peck so that the relevant member can spend much of the following day tucked away inside clothing, not needing to be pulled out whenever possible for inappropriate public display. A well loved Penis can rest happy knowing that he is a fully appreciated member of a loving relationship. ....and other such nonsense, please use your imaginations here.

The point of these kinds of games is that they are to convert the image of a penis into a playful thing to have fun with and to remove its fearsome reputations as ravagers and weapon or symbol of power.

The penis is full of fun filled possibilities, other than sex, for its opposite number, and developing this relationship deepens other aspects of the rest of the full intimate adult relationship.

This helps to integrate the penis into the fun time of a relationship instead of keeping it solely for the passionate times only.

I can't help thinking there would be less macho posturing and violence towards others, or even supremacy based on gender, if the penis was seen differently, as a sweet little bath toy rather than a symbol of difference and a weapon of power or status.

There would also be more equality between the sexes if we didn't see the owning of a penis as a mark of dominance which excuses its PTU from doing domestic chores, although I know most western men nowadays are happy to join in there are still some who think it is women's work, not theirs, because they have a penis!

And finally … although most of this has been said, dotted through this piece of writing, my aim is to change the conversation about the penis away from the negative ones, including the somewhat misandric view of certain groups of feminists and general (although often justified) man- haters in society.

It is important to develop a well understood role which the penis can play in a fully integrated world where no-one is exploited by anyone else on any level, sexually or in other form.

There are many wonderful well mannered pens out there. Wouldn't it be even more wonderful if they and their transportations units were able to encourage all men to drop the damaging ideologies they have embraced historically and fully incorporate the more mystical qualities of feminine energy and sexuality into their own lives so that everyone benefits fully!

I believe that opening up the debate on so many fronts, as this book does, and with love and humour as well as a scattering of just a few of the strong and highly political issues, we can move globally one step closer to this vision of loving harmony and full human equality.

My own experience of later life, that I hold so dear myself, and live within on a personal level with huge gratitude and astonishment that this can even be possible, given my personal history.

I want that for everybody if they want it for themselves and why wouldn't they? But whatever you want just make sure that absolutely nobody else is being hurt in the process

I never thought I could reach this place of happiness and if I can do it then so can anybody else. Each journey starts with the first step and that is to be open to rethinking it all.

This way we can also help to heal those whose journeys have left them damaged and either victims of abuse, or those seen as abusers.

There are many ways to end abuse but I believe this is a positive and lovingly constructive one to take, to heal a planet of humans whose greatest gift is so thoroughly distorted by misunderstandings based on historical ignorance and power. This is a time of change for all.

50% of all profits made from this book will go to charities working to end the sex trafficking of women and children.

42519786R00063

Printed in Poland
by Amazon Fulfillment
Poland Sp. z o.o., Wrocław